Shelby's Imagination Station

written by
Shelley Sleeper

illustrated by
Morgan Ann Hass

This book is dedicated to my amazing husband who gave me the courage to make not only my dream of becoming an author come true, but all of my dreams come true!
-SJS

I would like to dedicate this to my father for seeing this coming long before I did, and to Shelley Sleeper for the opportunity to make her dreams come to life.
-MAH

Designed by Francisco Macias O
Co-designed and Illustrated by Morgan Ann Hass

Published by Happy Everything LLC

Printed by Golden Cup

18 17 16 15 14 13 12   10 9 8 7 6 5 4 3 2

Hi! I'm Shelby! I'm 8-years old
and I'm in the second grade.
I love to do lots of different things.

I enjoy having play dates with my friends,
helping my mom and dad make dinner,
and I LOVE to take dance lessons!

But my favorite thing to do is use my imagination.

Using my imagination is the BEST because I get to imagine being anything I can think of!

This is my Imagination Station!

I made it from the box our new refrigerator came in.

Every time I learn about, think about, or experience something new, I jump into my Imagination Station and become it!

Things happen to me all the time
that give me ideas
for my Imagination Station.
Like the time I went to the zoo,
I imagined that I was a zookeeper.

DOWNTOWN

WASHINGTON
SEA-0821

Or the time my family and I rode
on the city bus to go downtown,
I imagined what it would be like
to be a city bus driver.

Today at school Mrs. Morris told us that we can be ANYTHING we want when we grow up.
(I already knew that!)

Tonight, our assignment is to write about
what we imagine being when we grow up.
I imagine being different things all the time...
How am I going to pick just one?

My dad always tells me I'm smart,
I love looking at the stars,
I AM really good at drawing... So many choices!

Wow, using my Imagination Station
really helped me imagine what it
would be like to be a teacher! Now I know exactly
what I am going to write for my assignment!

Shelby

I want to be a teacher when I grow up. I **LOVE** all the things teachers do!

1. Help kids learn
2. Correct papers
3. Go to meetings
4. Talk to the principal
5. Help kids with their problems
6. Go to RECESS!!!

Today I think being a teacher is the right career for me
but with so many choices and
my Imagination Station who knows what I'll choose
to be by the time I'm a grown-up!

As for the rest of the day,
I think I'll just stick to being an 8-year old!

Dear Parents,

Learning to read either comes naturally or it comes with challenges. These challenges can bring negative feelings toward reading. Throughout both my teaching career and master's education, I found that kids who don't love to read are likely the ones who find it difficult. Typically, the difficulties surround decoding the letters or understanding what they are reading, or both.

From over a decade of hands-on experience, I have found that it takes two things to change a child's attitude about reading. First, a child needs to have positive and successful experiences with reading. Secondly, they need to read things that are interesting to them.

To have positive experiences with reading, a reader must be able to accurately decode 95% of the text and comprehend what they are reading. One way to improve accuracy is to read the same text repeatedly. By doing this the reader gets familiar with the text and their accuracy improves. Stopping throughout the story to discuss what is happening and explaining any unfamiliar words will improve comprehension.

My hope is that by you and your child talking about Shelby's Imagination Station, your child's reading comprehension will improve, and that you'll both love this story enough to read it over and over again!

Happy Reading!

Shelley Sleeper

Comprehension Questions

Before you read the book:

- Ask your child to make a prediction about what the story may be about based on the title and cover of the book.

- With your child, go through the entire story ONLY looking at the pictures. Talk about who the characters are, where the story takes place, and what's happening. This will help your child comprehend the story when you read it.

During the story, stop and ask these questions:

- Do you like to do any of the activities that Shelby likes to do?

- What is an "imagination"?

- What does "experience" mean?

- Have you ever been to the zoo?

- Have you ever been on a city bus?

- What does "assignment" mean?

- Do you think Shelby likes her teacher? Why?

- What other things do teachers do?

- Do you remember what "assignment" means?

- Would you want to be a teacher when you grow up?

After you've read the book:

- Who were the characters in the story?

- Where did the story take place?

- What was the main idea?

- What are some characteristics that would describe Shelby?

- Could you make an Imagination Station at your house? What would you use to make it?

- Did you like the story? Why?

- What was your favorite part?

Here are some facts about teachers!

- They have a strong self-esteem.
- They are knowledgable about many subjects.
- They are good at thinking on their feet and improvising in a split second.
- They are warm and fun to be around.
- They are role models.
- They are flexible and easygoing.
- They get weekends and holidays off!
- They get summer vacation!
- Most of all, they LOVE kids!

If you want to become a teacher...
here are some facts about what it takes!

- Get great grades all throughout elementary school, middle school, high school, and college.
- Ask your teacher if you can help do things around the classroom.
- Start a journal. Write down things you see your teachers doing, things they say, and projects you would like to do with your students when you become a teacher.
- Volunteer in a classroom of a grade you would like to teach.
- Be respectful to everyone you meet.
- Be committed to your dream of becoming a teacher.
- Attend a college or university that has a teaching program.
- When it is time to apply for a job, personally deliver your resumé to schools where you would like to teach. This will give you the opportunity to make a personal connection with the principal and the secretary.

About the Author

When I was a kid, I wanted to be a teacher when I grew up. I always IMAGINED what it would be like... just like Shelby in this book. So after years of IMAGINING, I became an elementary school teacher. I taught my students how to use their IMAGINATIONS, and helped them believe they could be anything they IMAGINED being when they grew up.

Recently, I've spend a lot of time IMAGINING what it would be like to be a writer... IMAGINING where I would write, what I would write about, and how fun it would be. Using my IMAGINATION and believing in myself empowered me to become a writer!

I hope that after you read about Shelby and her adventures in her Imagination Station, you will also be empowered to follow your dreams!

Happy Reading!

Shelley Sleeper

About the Illustrator

I grew up in the Pacific Northwest and have lived in Seattle for seven years. I received my bachelor's degree at the University of Washington in English Literature.

I currently have a full-time marketing position as a writer at a Seattle-based software company, but have always had an avid passion for the arts. I love oil painting, mixed media collage, and photography, and am looking forward to exploring children's book illustrations and bringing the future adventures of Shelby and her Imagination Station to life.

Morgan Ann Hass